W9-DDC-907

ARNOLD LOBEL

Odd Owls & Stout Pigs

A Book of Nonsense

COLOR BY **ADRIANNE LOBEL**

HARPER

An Imprint of HarperCollins*Publishers*

E
LobeA

Library of Congress Cataloging-in-Publication Data

Lobel, Arnold.

    Odd owls & stout pigs : a book of nonsense / Arnold Lobel ; color by Adrianne Lobel. — 1st ed.

       p.   cm.

    Summary: Presents a linked collection of brief rhymes featuring owls and pigs.

    ISBN 978-0-06-180054-2 (trade bdg.) — ISBN 978-0-06-180055-9 (lib. bdg.)

    [1. Stories in rhyme.   2. Owls—Fiction.   3. Pigs—Fiction.]   I. Lobel, Adrianne, ill.   II. Title.

PZ8.3.L82Od   2009   2009001406

[E]—dc22   CIP

                                                                       AC

Typography by Martha Rago

09 10 11 12 13 LPR 10 9 8 7 6 5 4 3 2 1 ❖ First Edition

For Crosby and George

—Arnold Lobel

For Ruby and her grandfather

—Adrianne Lobel

· One ·

Owls Old and Odd

This owl blows up a big balloon.
He blows it till it breaks.
He doesn't mind at all because
He likes the pop it makes.

This owl is on a holiday.
He's jumping into lakes.
He's always very wet because
He likes the splash it makes.

While sitting at supper,
This owl makes a mess.
"I have ruined my appearance!"
He cries with distress.
"In spreading the butter
On top of my bread,
It seems I have buttered
My necktie instead."

The music critics
Are greatly impressed.
At playing piano,
This owl is the best.
He hits the right notes
And there's never one missed
While playing the music
Of Chopin and Liszt.
"It's clear," says this owl,
"Why I play with such ease.
I use only feathers
To tickle these keys."

This owl is in her garden
Just admiring her plants.
She is singing in her garden
And she does a little dance.
She is watering her garden,
Every daffodil and rose.
She's so happy in her garden
That she's wiggling her toes.

All around the circus ring
These clown owls do everything.
One wears a very baggy suit.
One drops down in a parachute.
One is standing on his head.
One is having lunch in bed.
One can balance cups and plates.
One zooms by on roller skates.
One is playing with a pig.
Another wears a Beatle wig.
One is quickly jumping rope.
One shampoos his feet with soap.
One is dancing with a cat.
One grows mushrooms on his hat.
One looks fine in Scottish kilts.
One is high above on stilts.
One is beating on a drum.
One is chewing bubble gum.
One clown owl is taking showers.
One is smelling pretty flowers.
One is very, very small.
Another owl is thin and tall.

Explore this picture carefully, for all these owls are here to see.

And if you really use your eyes, you'll find one owl is a surprise.

This is an owl who is very rich.
He never spends a dime.
He puts his pennies in high piles
And shines them all the time.
At night he tucks his coins in bed
With tender, loving care.
It gives him joy to see each cent
Asleep beside him there.

This owl is tossing in the air
A box of ice-cream cakes.
He's happy as a lark because
He likes the mess it makes.

This owl is eating sour balls
Until his stomach aches.
His chewing never stops because
He likes the crunch it makes.

This is an owl in an armchair.
It's where he always sits.
Sometimes he counts his scaly toes
And other times he knits.
His chair is covered beautifully
With flowers all entwined.
It's comfortable from every side,
In front and in behind.
If robbers come to steal this chair,
They'll learn some sorry news.
It's fastened to the floor, you see,
With eighty-nine large screws.

This owl is in a restaurant.
He's drinking ten milk shakes.
He drinks them with a straw because
He likes the slurp it makes.

This owl enjoys the wintertime,
The ice and white snowflakes.
He sleigh rides down the hill because
He likes the whiz it makes.

This owl plays music on a flute.
He's playing for some snakes.
Those snakes are twisting just because
They like the toot he makes.

This owl is speeding in his car.
He steps hard on the brakes.
He does this everywhere because
He likes the screech it makes.

•Two•

A Group of Stout Pigs

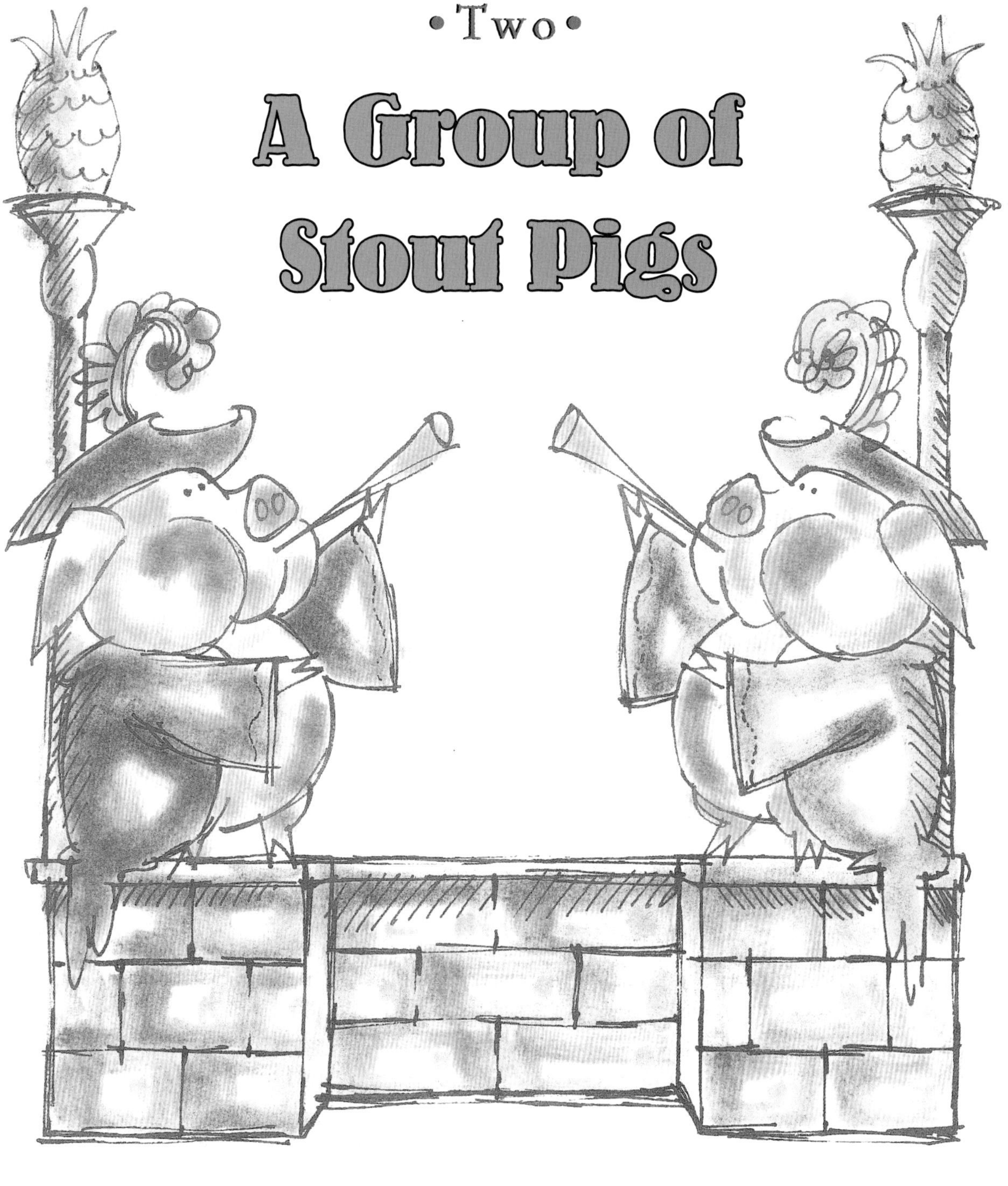

A pig from the isle of Nantucket
Went far out to sea in a bucket.
There he met a large fish
Who said, "Pig is my dish."
So he sailed quickly back to Nantucket.

There was a young pig from Hoboken
Who found that his wristwatch was broken.
He cried, "It's distressing
To always be guessing
The right time of day in Hoboken."

There was a small pig with a tail,
Not curly but straight as a nail.
So she ate simply oodles
Of pretzels and noodles,
Which put a nice twist to her tail.

"It's T minus one as I clock it,"
Said a pig astronaut in his rocket.
As he zoomed to the moon
He cried, "I'll be back soon,
With a piece of green cheese in my pocket."

There was a young pig who wept tears
When his mother said, "I'll wash your ears."
As she poured on the soap
He cried, "I truly hope
This won't happen again for ten years."

There was a pig lady from Maine
Who was caught in a strong hurricane.
But that lady just grinned
And cried, "I love the wind!"
As she flew high up over the plain.

Two pigs each night played their guitars,
Singing loud songs out under the stars.
But a man in a house
With cold water did douse
Those two pigs and their noisy guitars.

An unfortunate pig from Jamaica
Once made a most awful mistaka.
He stuck his round nose
In a dryer for clothes,
And it spun him right out of Jamaica.

There was a cowpig from the West
Who could shoot and chase bad men with zest.
When his bullets went flying,
The bandits were lying
In piles on the ground in the West.

There was an old pig from New York
Who ate without knife, spoon, or fork.
Each time he ate peas,
They rolled down to his knees,
Which upset that old pig from New York.

A group of stout pigs from Savannah
Once slipped on a peel of banana.
When those large pigs fell down,
Every person in town
Thought an earthquake had hit poor Savannah.

• • • Author's Note • • •

This book, *Odd Owls & Stout Pigs*, is made up of two of the three little handmade volumes that were discovered at the estate auction of George and Crosby Bonsall by Justin Schiller, a collector of rare and antique children's books. I have worked with Justin over the years on appraisals and placements of my papa's archives. Crosby and George were great friends of both my parents in the sixties and seventies, when these books were made by Papa as Christmas gifts for them.

When Justin showed me these books (which I had never seen before), I thought they should be taken out of storage where they had lain for forty years and brought to the public. I showed them to the editors at HarperCollins, where there was much excitement, and publication was put into motion instantly.

As relatively early works of Arnold Lobel, they are the amuse-bouches before the later entrées of the Frog and Toad stories, *Owl at Home*, and *The Book of Pigericks*. Meant for friends' eyes only, they show Papa's writing and illustration in a most casual and lively form.

My goal in coloring these sketches was to maintain the sense of joy and spontaneity that I found in the pictures. If the enjoyment that I received in working on both this book and *The Frogs and Toads All Sang* is any proof, then I have succeeded. I hope some of this pleasure will rub off on you—the reader.

Thank you,
Adrianne Lobel